A Children's Book About

OVERDOING IT

Managing Editor: Ellen Klarberg
Copy Editor: Annette Gooch
Editorial Assistant: Lana Eberhard
Art Director: Jennifer Wiezel
Production Artist: Gail Miller
Illustration Designer: Bartholomew
Inking Artist: Micah Schwaberow
Coloring Artists: Linda Hanney, Berenice Happé Iriks
Lettering Artist: Linda Hanney
Typographer: Communication Graphics

A Children's Book About

OVERDOING IT

By Joy Berry

GROLIER ENTERPRISES CORP.

This book is about Lennie.

Reading about Lennie can help you understand and deal with **overdoing it.**

You are overdoing it when you have too much of something. You are overdoing it when you do too much of something. Too much of anything can be harmful. When you overdo it, you can hurt yourself or others.

You can overdo it by *eating or drinking too much.* Try not to do this. Do these things instead:

- Take only a little bit of food at one time.
- Eat and drink slowly.
- Finish one mouthful of food before taking another.
- Do not eat so much that you feel stuffed.
- Do not eat too much of any one thing, especially sweets.

You can overdo it by *staying up too late* and *not getting enough sleep.*

Try not to stay up too late. Do these things instead:

- With your parent's approval, decide when you should go to bed.
- Give yourself at least half an hour before bedtime to get ready for bed.
- Go to bed on time. Do not put it off.

You can overdo it by *being around one person too much.*

Try not to be around any one person too much.

Have several playmates so that you will not have to play with one person all of the time.

Learn to play alone so that you can be by yourself when you need to be.

You can overdo it by *staying in one place too long.*

Try not to stay in any one place for too long.
Do these things instead:

- Go into another room if you have been in one room too long.
- Go outside if you have been inside too long.
- Go to a playground or to a friend's house if you have been at home too much.

You can overdo it by *doing something too much*. For example, you can overdo it by watching too much TV.

Try not to watch too much TV. Do these things instead:

- With the help of your parents, decide which TV programs you should watch.
- Turn on the TV only when it is time for one of these programs. Turn off the TV when the program is over.
- Try not to watch TV for more than one or two hours at a time.

You can overdo it by *being too rough.*

Try not to be rough with things. Do this instead:

- Find out how to use things properly.
- Use things the way they should be used.

SIGH!
MOM WAS RIGHT. I SHOULDN'T BE SO ROUGH WITH MY THINGS.
YEAH! ESPECIALLY YOUR CAT!

You can overdo it by *playing too roughly with other people.* Playing too roughly can cause someone to get hurt. This is why you should avoid playing roughly with others.

It is important to not overdo it so you can enjoy the wonderful people, places, and things around you.